First published as Jonnie in Belgium and Holland by Clavis Uitgeverij, Hasselt—Amsterdam, 2012
English translation from the Dutch by Clavis Publishing Inc., New York

Visit us on the Web at www.clavisbooks.com.

Johnny written and illustrated by Guido van Genechten

ISBN 978-1-60537-377-5 (hardback edition)
ISBN 978-1-60537-394-2 (paperback edition)

This book was printed in March 2018 at DENONA d.o.o., Zagreb, Marina Getaldica 1, Croatia.

First Edition
10 9 8 7 6 5 4 3 2 1

Clavis Publishing supports the First Amendment and celebrates the right to read.

Johnny

Guido van Genechten

Clavis

NEW YORK

Johnny was a very sweet spider . . .
. . . but nobody knew it!

Because wherever **Johnny** went,
everyone ran screaming
out the door...

...before he could even say "I..."

"Eeek!
A stinky, prickly beast,"
the grasshopper screamed,
and he jumped far away...

"Aaack!
A black-haired monster!"
the bee yelled, and
she whizzed off . . .

"**Eek**,
an itchy-scratchy thing,"
the butterfly yelled, and
he fluttered high in the sky . . .

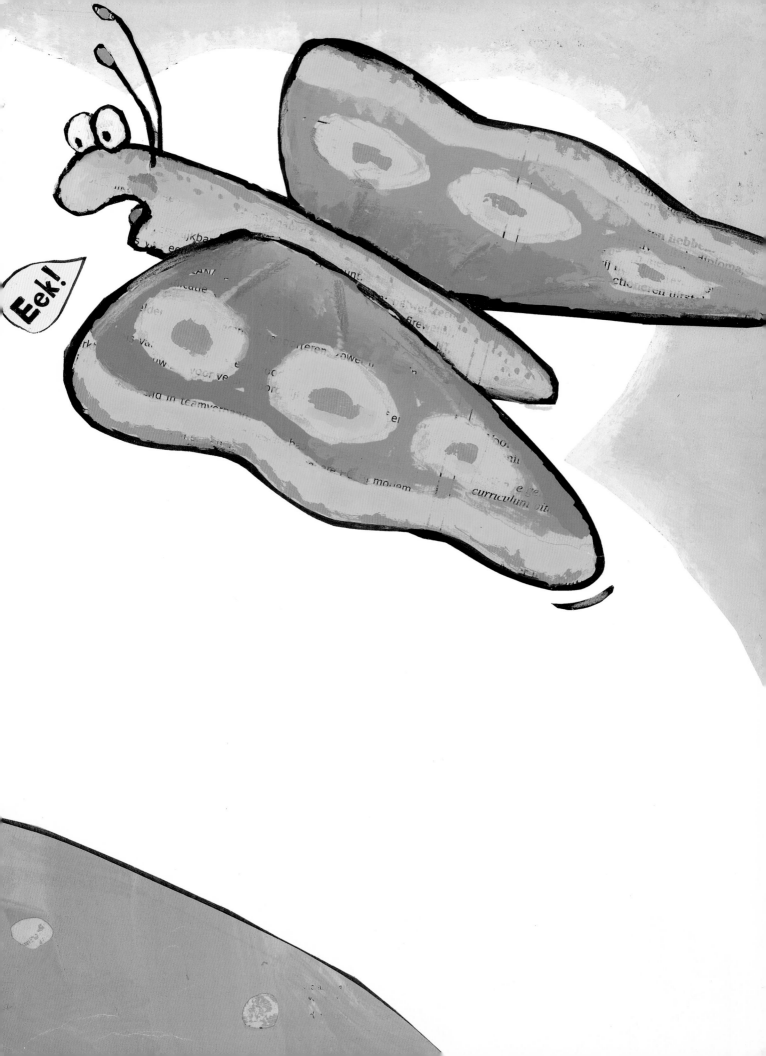

"Ugh,
a filthy,
fat slimeball,"
the snail screamed,

and she fled back into
her little house . . .

"Yuck!
An awfully ugly creep,"
the worm cried,
and he quickly dove
back under the ground...

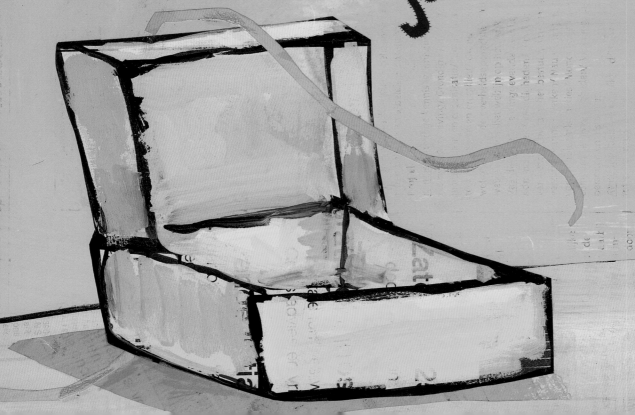

And he
ate the cake
all by himself.
Gulp!

Johnny is a very sweet spider, but nobody knows that . . .

Except you!

So if you see **Johnny** around,
give him a very big kiss.